D0386682

OLIVIA™
and the Rain Dance

adapted by Maggie Testa
based on the screenplay "Olivia Makes it Rain"
written by Michael Stern
illustrated by Guy Wolek

Ready-to-Read

Simon Spotlight
New York   London   Toronto   Sydney   New Delhi

Based on the TV series *OLIVIA*™ as seen on Nickelodeon™

SIMON SPOTLIGHT

An imprint of Simon & Schuster Children's Publishing Division

1230 Avenue of the Americas, New York, New York 10020

For information about special discounts for bulk purchases, please contact Simon & Schuster Special Sales at
1-866-506-1949 or business@simonandschuster.com.

Manufactured in the United States of America 1211 LAK

First Edition

1 2 3 4 5 6 7 8 9 10

ISBN 978-1-4424-3542-1 (pbk)

ISBN 978-1-4424-3543-8 (hc)

ISBN 978-1-4424-4718-9 (eBook)

Olivia, Ian, and Francine
are going to the park.
They will have a boat race.

"Hey, where is the water?"
asks Ian.

"It has not rained in weeks,"
says Mr. Greengrass.
"It might not rain again
for a long time."

"If only I could control the weather," says Olivia.
That gives Olivia an idea.
"I wonder . . ."

"We can make it rain!"
she says.
Olivia, Francine, and Ian
dress up for a rain dance.

"Just do what I do,"
says Olivia.
"Reach to the sky!"

Now spin like a top!"

"And now just do whatever you want!" says Olivia.

Drip, drop!

"It is working!" cries Olivia.

"It is only Ian,"
says Francine.
But Ian gives Olivia an idea.

"We can fill up the pond with the hose," she says. Olivia, Ian, and Francine pull . . . and pull . . . and pull.

But the hose is not long
enough.

"Pull harder," says Olivia.

Francine drops the hose.
Olivia and Ian go flying!
"Oops, sorry!" cries
Francine.

Olivia has another idea—
water balloons!
"How will we get all these
water balloons to the pond?"
asks Francine.

Olivia smiles.
She knows just what to do.
"Ready! Aim! Fire!"
she commands.

Splat!

"We cannot have a boat race without water," says Ian.

Olivia sees Connor go by
on his skateboard.
She knows just what to do!
"We can have a
boat race without water!"

"Follow me!" says Olivia.

"Welcome to Olivia's first
annual toy boat race—
on dry land!" says Olivia.

Go, Ian!
Go, Francine!
Go, Olivia!

It is a three-way tie!

Then *boom*!

It starts to thunder.

Then it starts to rain.

It is still raining
at bedtime.
Olivia smiles.
They can have a
water boat race tomorrow.